The k

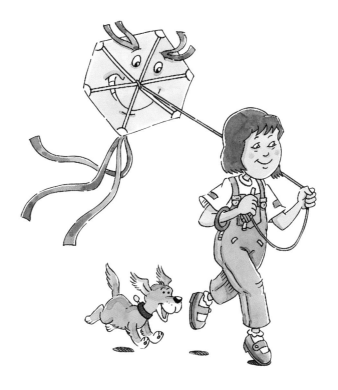

Illustrated by Kelvin Hawley

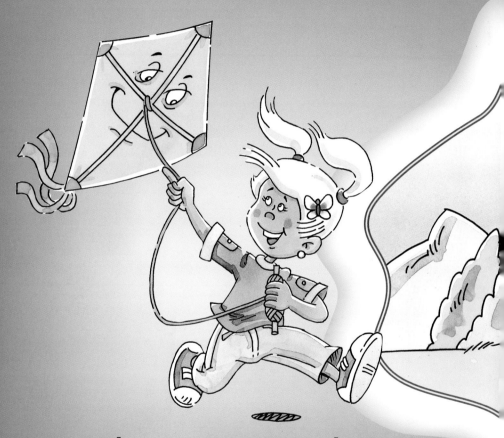

The green kite
is going up.

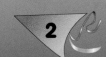

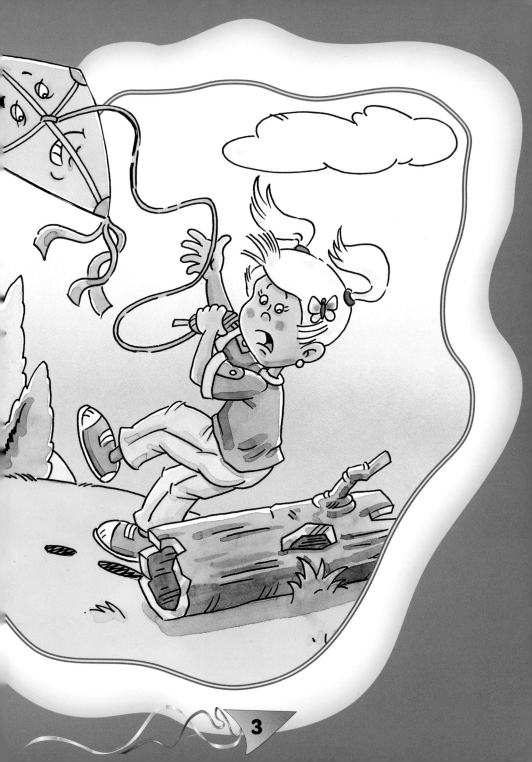

3

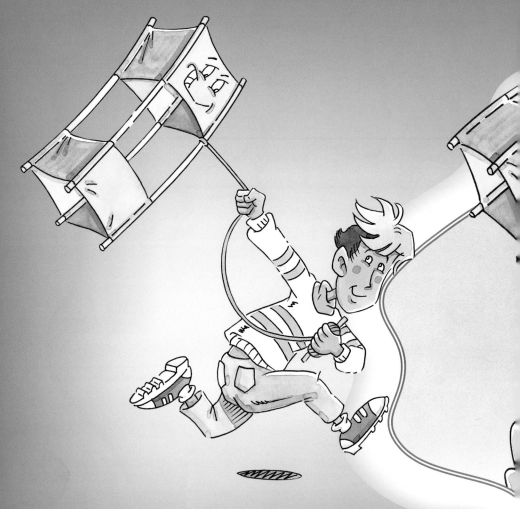

The blue kite is going up.

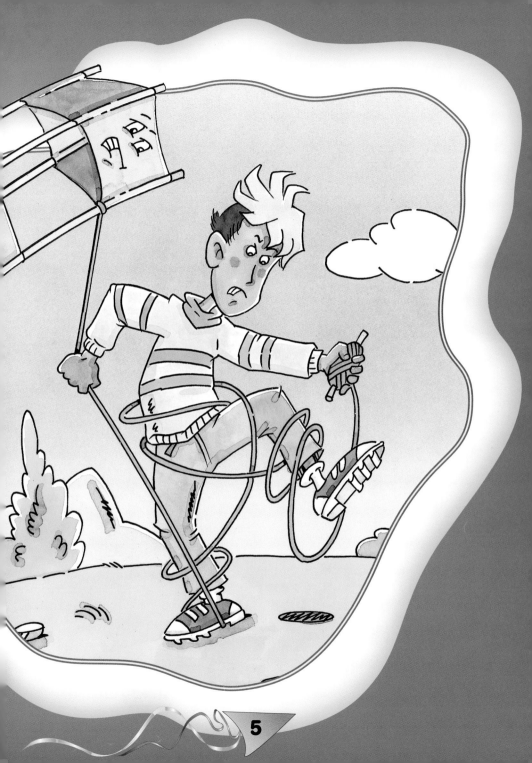

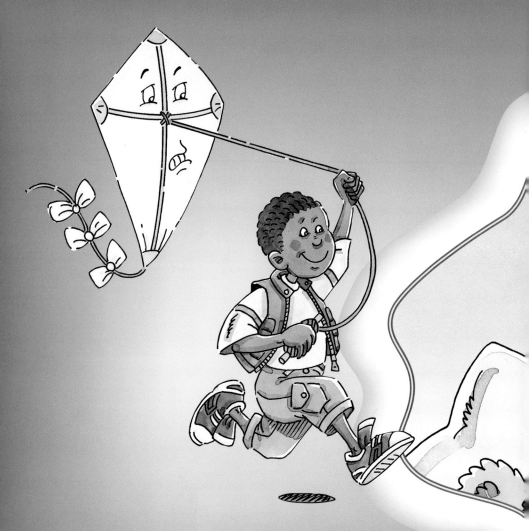

The yellow kite
is going up.

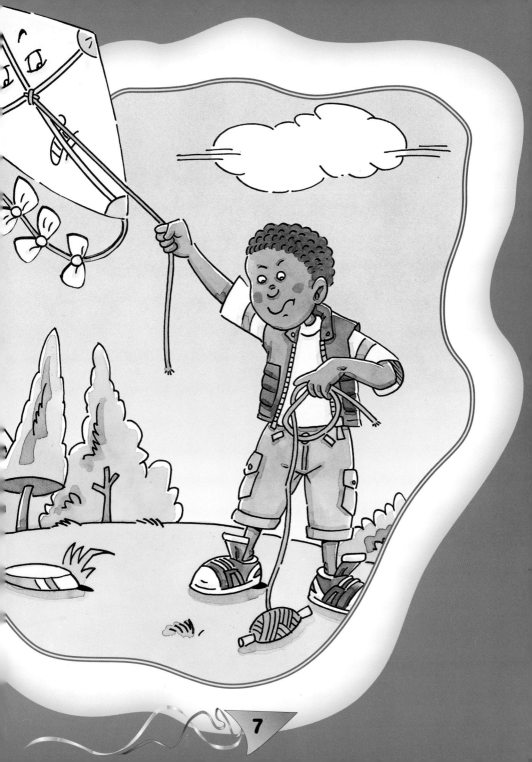

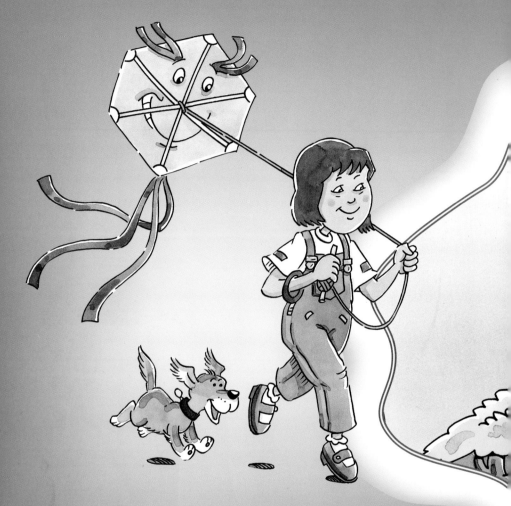

The purple kite
is going up.

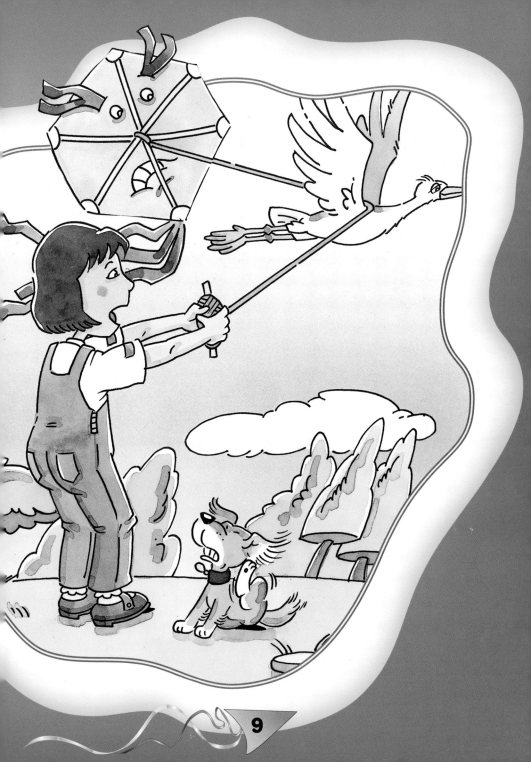

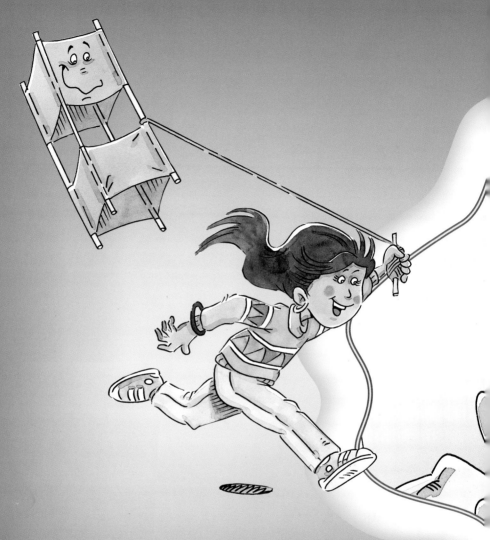

The pink kite
is going up.

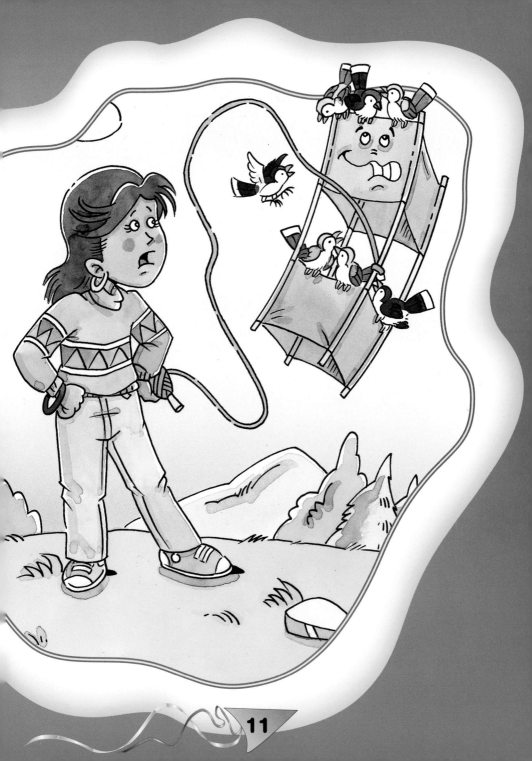

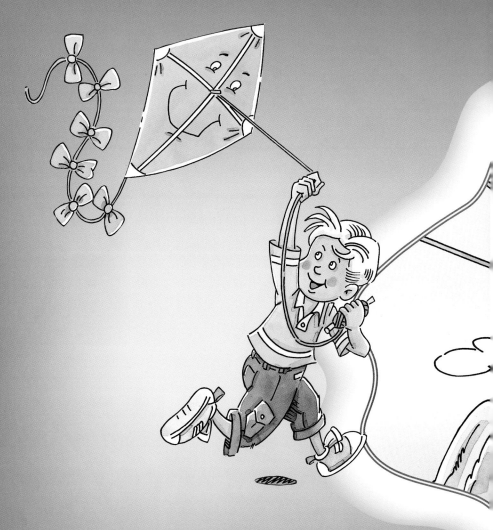

The orange kite
is going up.

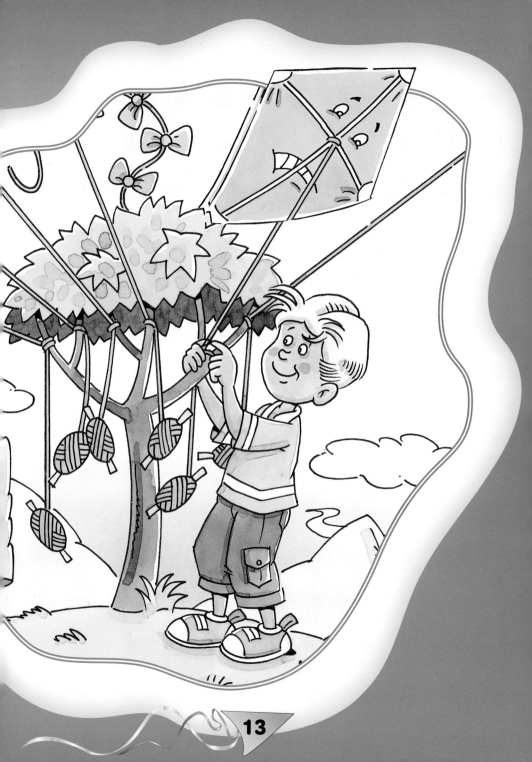

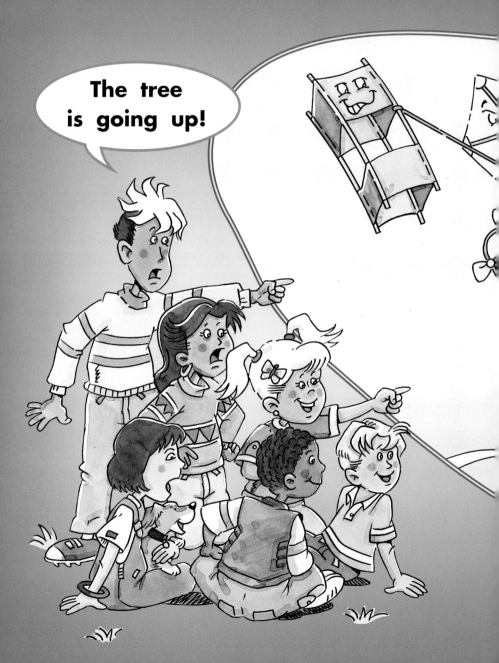

14

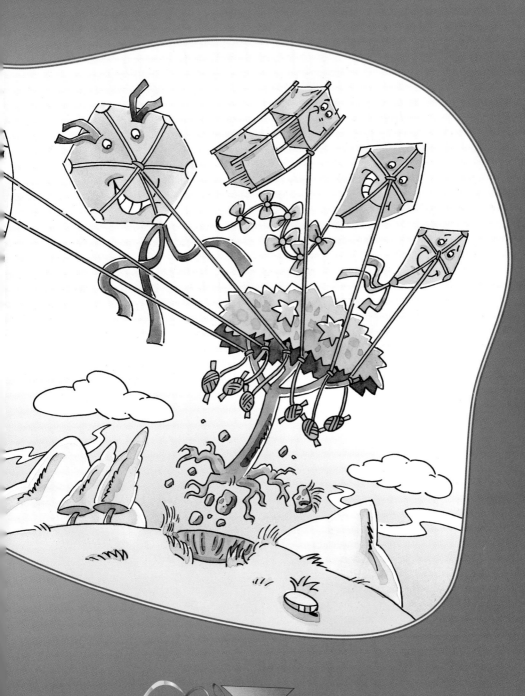

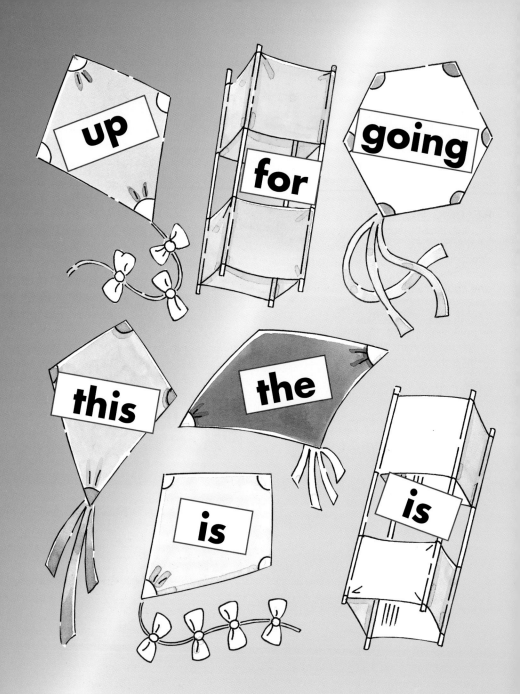